Other books by Mick Inkpen:

One Bear at Bedtime
Threadbear
Billy's Beetle
Penguin Small
Lullabyhullaballoo!
Nothing
Bear
The Great Pet Sale

The Wibbly Pig books
The Kipper books
The Blue Nose Island books

First published in 1989
by Hodder Children's Books,
a division of Hachette Children's Books
338 Euston Road, London NW1 3BH

Text and illustrations copyright © Mick Inkpen 1989

This edition published in 2006
10 9 8 7 6 5 4 3
ISBN-10: 0340 918195
ISBN-13: 9780340 918197

A CIP catalogue record for this book
is available from the British Library.

Manufactured in China

The Blue Balloon

MICK INKPEN

Hodder
Children's
Books

A division of Hachette Children's Books

The day after my birthday party
Kipper found a soggy blue balloon
in the garden.

It was odd because the balloons
at my party were red and white.

I blew it up.

At first I thought it was
just an ordinary balloon.
But now I am not so sure.

It is shiny and squeaky and
you can make rude noises with it.
And if you give it a rub you can
stick it on the ceiling.
Just like an ordinary balloon.

But there is something odd about my balloon.

It doesn't matter how much you blow it up, it just goes on getting bigger . . .

You see it never ever bursts. Never ever.

I have squeezed it . . .   squashed it . . .

. . . and whacked it with a stick.

I have kicked it . . .   run it over . . .

. . . and stretched it!

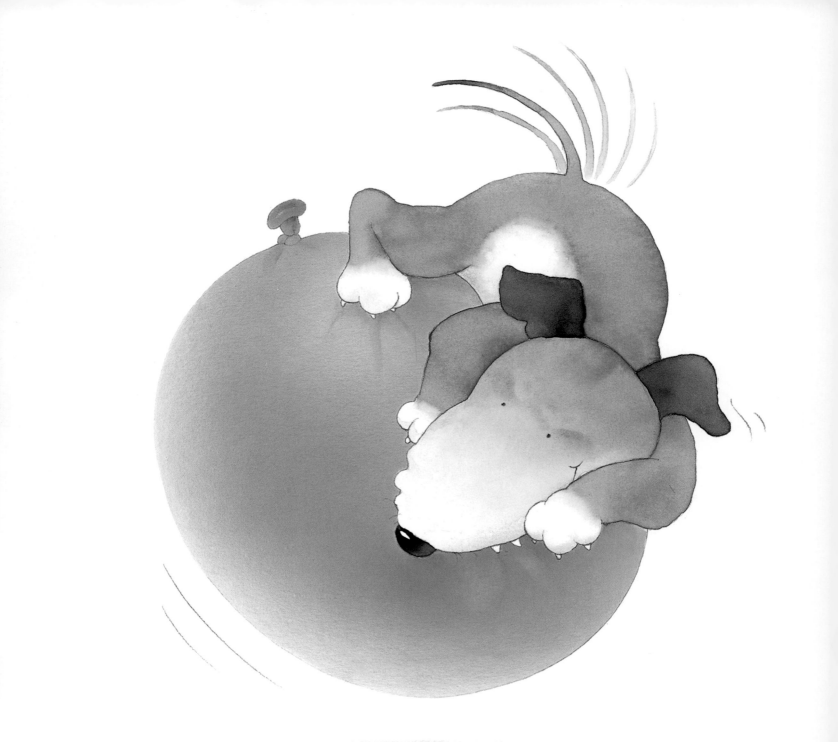

And Kipper has attacked it.
But it is Indestructible.

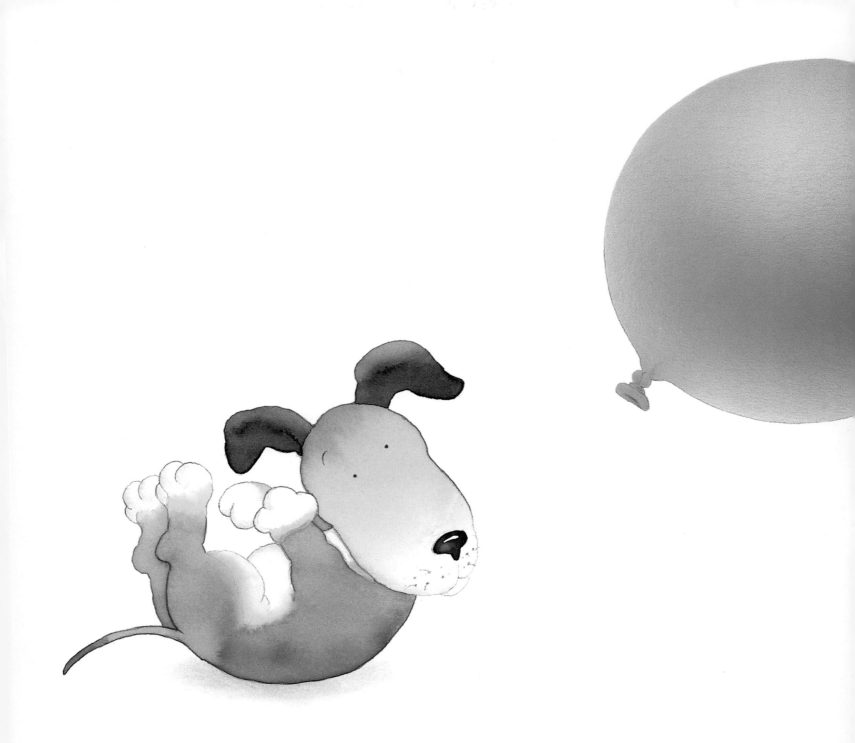

I think that my balloon has
Strange and Wonderful Powers!

The other day it disappeared completely . . .

. . . and when it came back it was square!

And this morning, while I was taking it for a walk . . .

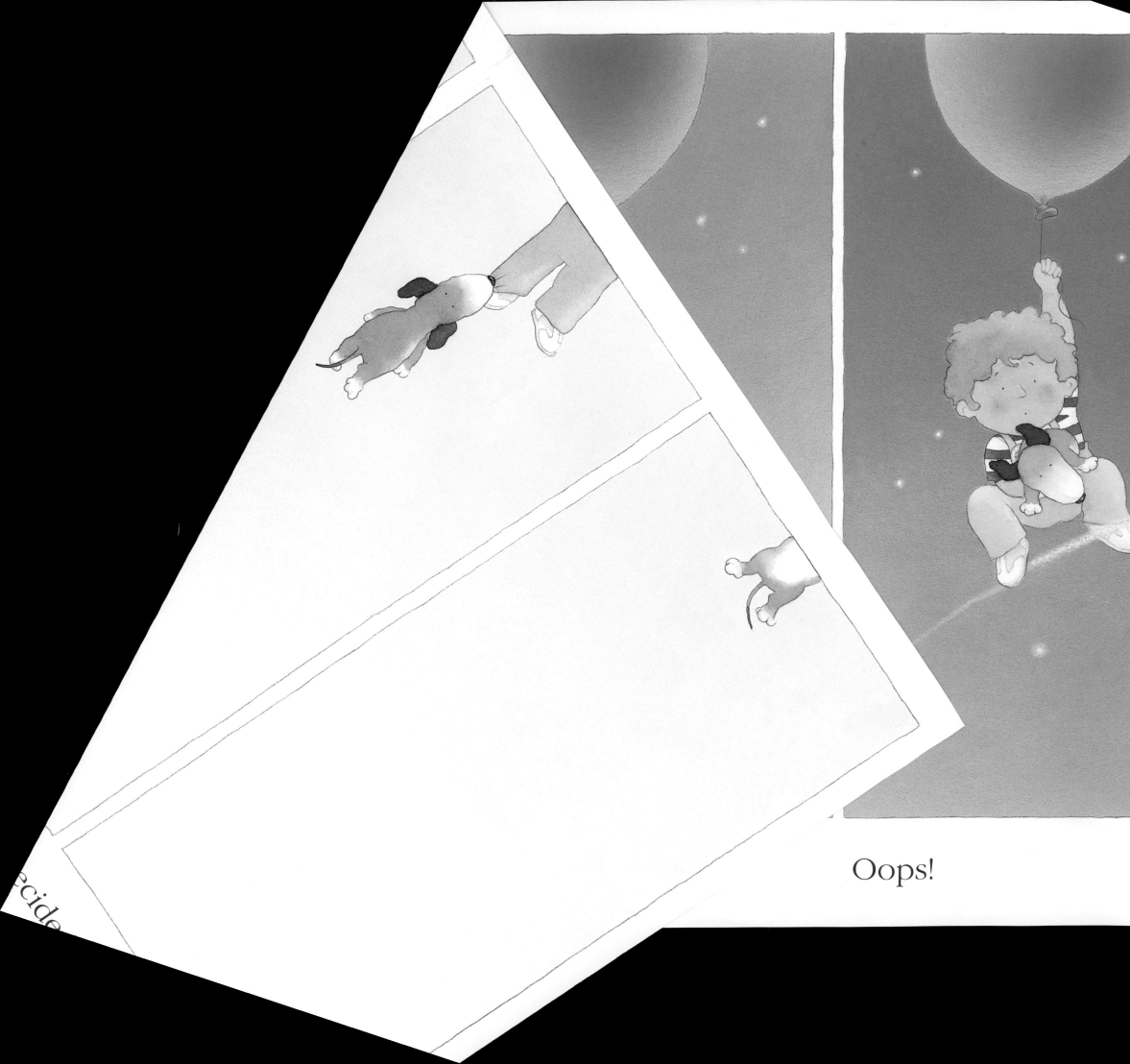

Oops!

And finally . . .   . . . down.

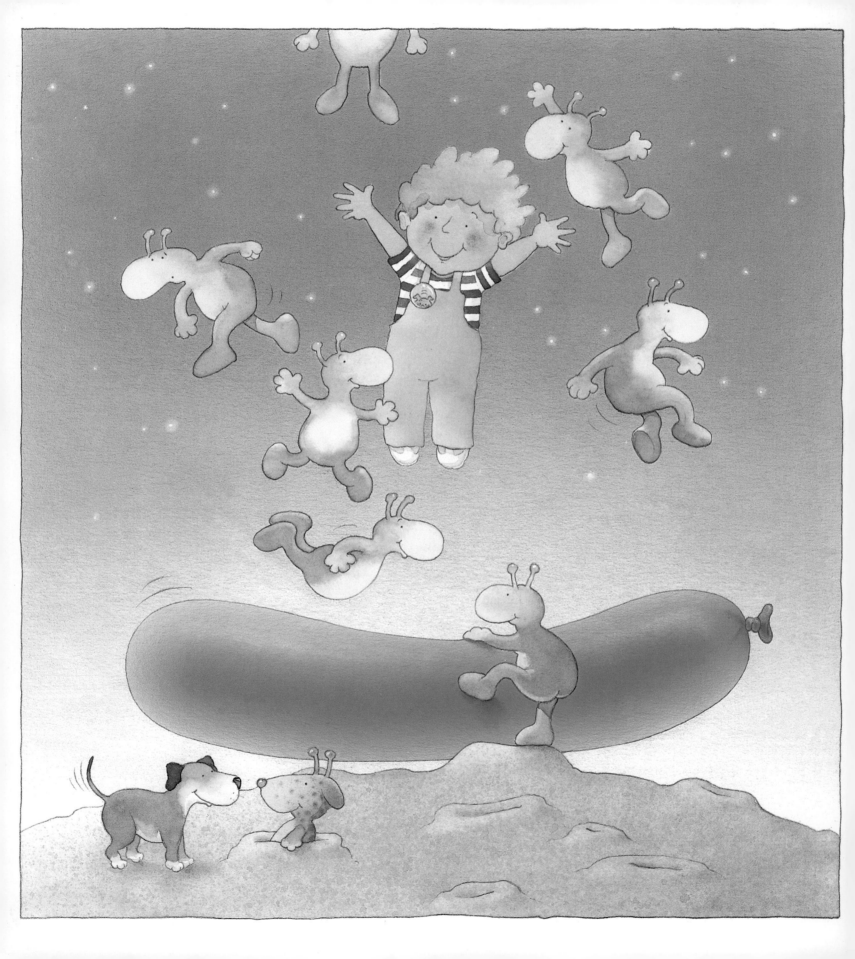

It was quite a trip, but we
were back in time for tea.

So if you find a soggy old balloon . . .

. . . whatever you do
don't throw it away.

Especially if it's a blue one.

You never know what it will do next.